A Fish in a Tree

DEBORAH C. WASHINGTON
CHAD THOMPSON

A Fish in a Tree

Published by Purple Diamond Press, LLC 2021
Copyright © 2021 by Deborah C. Washington

Written by Deborah C. Washington
Illustrated by Chad Thompson
Edited by Jennifer Rees

Paperback: ISBN: 978-163918997-7

Library of Congress Control Number: 2021915687
Villa Park, CA

Visit www.DCWashingtonBooks.com for more information
This book can be purchased directly from the publisher.
Special discount for large quantities for schools/organizations.
Info@PurpleDiamondPress.com
www.PurpleDiamondPress.com

DEDICATION

For my grandchildren; Jeremiah, Kayden, Arielle,
Arianna, Silas, and Zion, and any future grandchildren.
May you all always be respectful and thankful for
the amazing earth that God has given us.
Thank you to George, my husband, for his
encouragement. Finally, a special thank you to
Silas, for his enthusiasm and inspiration for this
story—without you, this story would not exist.

- - -

I would like to thank the talented team that
has made this book become a reality.
My deepest gratitude to Charity Harris,
Jennifer Rees and Chad Thompson.
I am blessed to have found you all.

"Hey, what is that up in my tree?"

Twitchy Squirrel wondered, "Can you see?

A green and blue fish up in my tree.

Flipping and flopping—how can that be?"

"What?" said Wren. "That can't be true!
I'll check it out." And up she flew.
Twitchy scampered up the tree, too,
Getting himself a better view.

"We were fooled, Twitchy, have no fear—
It's a fish-shaped balloon, way up here.
Who would think a fish could be so near?
And how did it ever get way up here?"

"Maybe someone didn't hold on tight,
Or maybe, despite all their might,
The string slipped; the balloon took flight...
And drifted up, up out of sight."

"The wind blew it far, far away,

Over houses and kids at play.

It landed here, but it can't stay.

Let's work together, what do you say?"

"Yes, it's pretty, but it can't stay.

If there's no one to take it away,

It becomes litter, I've heard them say.

Let's get it down from this tree today."

Twitchy clawed at the string wound tight,

and Wren pecked with all her might.

The string got loose, but the fish took flight.

"Oh, no, it's flying out of sight!"

"I'll be back," said Wren. "Bye, bye."

She followed the fish up, up high.

A funny sight for anyone to spy,

A bird following a fish up in the sky.

The balloon landed in the sea,

Just the right place for a fish to be.

But a balloon is not a fish, you see,

And never, ever belongs in the sea.

The flattened fish washed up on the shore,

Not looking like a balloon anymore,

Tangled in an old wooden oar.

Wren feared this was worse than before.

Three curious turtles swam closer to see.

The older one said, "Stop, please listen to me.

Strings can be a danger for us," said he.

They swam away, fast as turtles can flee.

Kicking up sand, a boy came around.

He picked up the fish. "Look what I found!"

It was wet and twisted. He put it back down.

"Wait," said his mom, "we can't litter the ground."

"It was cool-looking before, it's true.

Do you remember what we need to do?"

"Reuse, recycle, or renew."

"You are right, what shall we do?"

"I know! Can I take it home with me?"

"It depends on what your plan will be."

"I'll clean it up. That's what I'll do!

And hang it in my room, like new."

"You chose renew—I'm sure you can.

Let's take it home with that plan.

Your thoughts are creative, my young man.

Take care of the earth however you can."

As Wren looked down, she wasn't sure
But thought the fish had winked at her!
Things had worked out in the end.
Off she flew to tell her friend.

About The Author

From the moment Deborah won an essay contest in 3rd grade, she has loved writing. She since then was an editor for a small-town paper for two years, and two-time winner of Connecticut Authors and Publishers short story contest. Also, a poetry award winner, Deborah has had numerous articles and stories published in newspapers and other publications.

Deborah had a career with the United States Postal Service for 34 years, the last 17 as a Postmaster while she and her husband raised their two children. Now a retired grandmother, she is spending more time on her love of writing and focuses on recycling and repurposing. Deborah has always been concerned about the danger of balloons for wildlife when intentionally released and wants to share the importance of saving our beautiful planet with young readers.

DCWashingtonBooks.com

Deborah and her family take action in keeping our planet safe and clean.